EPIC
ADVENTURES

Written by Julia March

DK | Penguin Random House

Senior Editor Selina Wood
Designer Elena Jarmoskaite
Pre-production Producer Marc Staples
Producer Louise Daly
Managing Editor Paula Regan
Managing Art Editor Jo Connor
Publisher Julie Ferris
Art Director Lisa Lanzarini
Publishing Director Simon Beecroft

Reading Consultant Linda B. Grambell, Ph.D.

First American Edition, 2019
Published in the United States by DK Publishing
1450 Broadway, Suite 801, New York, NY 10018

Page design copyright © 2019 Dorling Kindersley Limited
DK, a Division of Penguin Random House LLC
19 20 21 22 23 10 9 8 7 6 5 4 3 2 1
001–313927–Aug/2019

A catalog record for this book is available from the Library of Congress.

ISBN: 978-1-4654-8426-0 (Paperback)
ISBN: 978-1-4654-8427-7 (Hardback)

DK books are available at special discounts when purchased in bulk for
sales promotions, premiums, fund-raising, or educational use. For details, contact:
DK Publishing Special Markets, 1450 Broadway,
Suite 801, New York, NY 10018

SpecialSales@dk.com

Printed and bound in China

A WORLD OF IDEAS:
SEE ALL THERE IS TO KNOW

www.dk.com
www.LEGO.com

Contents

Ninja on guard

Ninjago Island is a land of mountains, forests, towns, and temples. It is a magical place, but not a peaceful one. Many villains want to conquer Ninjago and rule over its people.

Cole

Lloyd

Jay

Kai

Six brave ninja defend Ninjago against these threats. Their names are Cole, Jay, Lloyd, Kai, Zane, and Nya. The ninja train hard to strengthen their bodies and minds. They are guided by their teacher, Master Wu.

Master Wu

Zane

Nya

The ninja use an ancient martial art known as Spinjitzu. Every day, they gather for their training session. Lloyd, Jay, Zane, Nya, Cole, and Kai are all eager to work hard.

Training is not just about building strong muscles. The ninja must also develop quick thinking and fast reactions. They must learn to handle all kinds of weapons, too.

The ninja training arena is called a dojo. Master Wu watches the ninja carefully as they train. This wise old teacher has years of experience as a ninja coach.

The ninja are skilled at using
many weapons, but each of them has
a favorite. Nya uses her spear to battle
enemies and sometimes to vault over
them. Zane throws his three-pointed
shurikens to stop enemy vehicles.
Kai has a special Sword of Fire that
shoots fireballs to drive off foes.

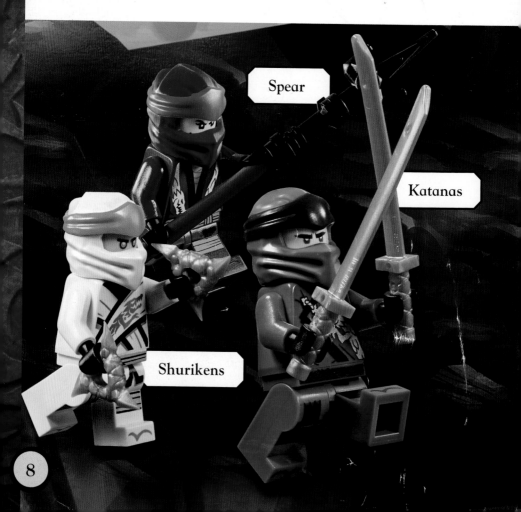

Spear

Katanas

Shurikens

Nunchuck

Scythe

Sword of Fire

Jay whirls his nunchuck around so fast it gives out bursts of electricity. Cole has a scythe sharp enough to cut through stone. As for Lloyd, he wields not one but two golden katanas. He is equally skilled with his right and left hands.

Whatever the adventure, the ninja have a perfect vehicle for it. When Kai steals the Sword of Fire from the Venomari snakes, he uses his Blade Cycle to make a getaway. When the snakes catch up with him, Kai flips up the blades on the cycle so the snakes have to back off!

Kai's Blade Cycle

Jay's Storm Fighter looks like an ordinary plane, but when it flies into action enemies had better take cover.

Jay's Storm Fighter

The Storm Fighter's wings suddenly fold out—and they are loaded with weapons.

Cole's Dirt Bike can power over sand with its caterpillar treads. It is also armed with weapons.

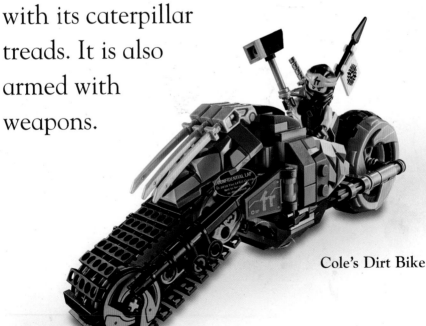
Cole's Dirt Bike

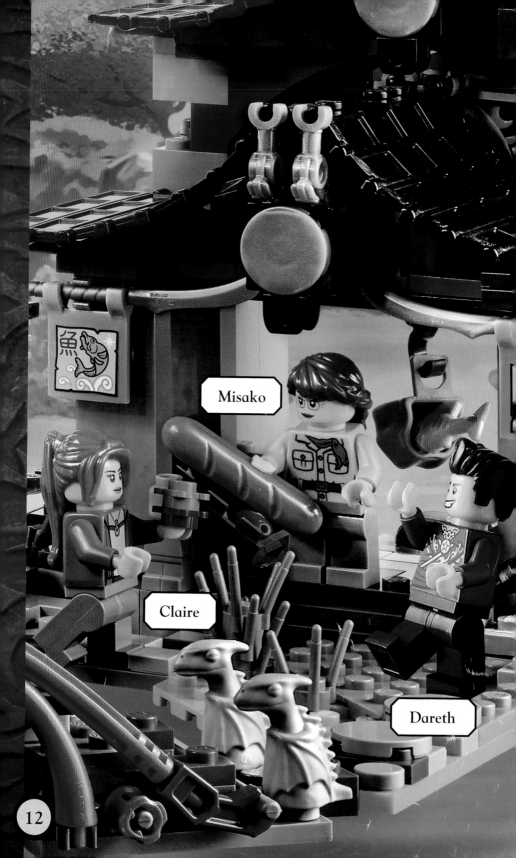

Misako

Claire

Dareth

12

The ninja have many friends who support them in their mission to defend Ninjago. Dareth is a karate expert. He longs to be a ninja like his friends, but lacks the special skills.

Ronin

Misako is Lloyd's mom. She wishes the ninja did not have to keep fighting Lord Garmadon. Before he turned bad, he was her loving husband!

Ronin was once a bounty hunter, paid to chase down the ninja. Now he is their ally and fights alongside them.

Lots of ordinary folk help the ninja, too. Claire doesn't have ninja skills, but she likes to visit their Temple.

Dragons are born in the First Realm, a place older than Ninjago itself. Firstbourne is the oldest dragon. People call her the "Mother of all Dragons." If Firstbourne senses good in someone, she helps them. She carries Kai into battle against Garmadon, with her dragon army following behind.

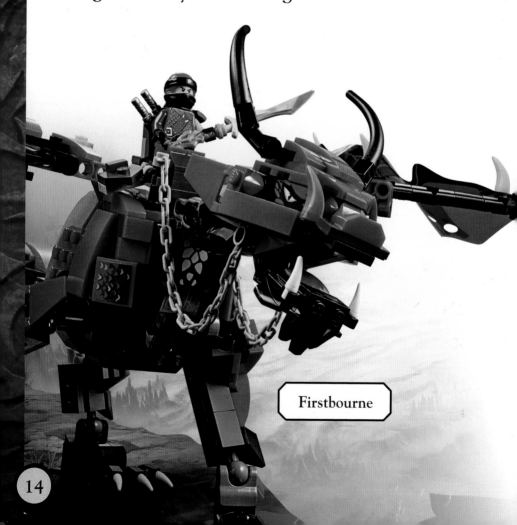

Firstbourne

Stormbringer

Each ninja rides a dragon linked
to their own powers. Jay's dragon
is Stormbringer, a fast-flying beast.
Instead of breathing fire, Stormbringer
breathes crackling bolts of lightning.
They give enemies a nasty shock!

Each of the six ninja has a special Elemental Power. They use these powers to protect Ninjago Island from enemies.

Name: Cole
Element: Earth
Power: He can create earthquakes and mountains. He stops foes by piling dirt on them.

Name: Jay
Element: Lightning
Power: He creates bolts of electricity that zap anything they hit.

Name: Kai
Element: Fire
Power: He fires bursts of flames to melt his foes' weapons or turn their vehicles to ash.

Name: Zane
Element: Ice
Power: He fires powerful ice blasts at his enemies. He can trap them in blocks of ice, too.

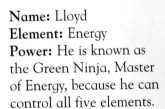

Name: Nya
Element: Water
Power: She creates rain, waves, and waterspouts. She also uses water jets to fly.

Name: Lloyd
Element: Energy
Power: He is known as the Green Ninja, Master of Energy, because he can control all five elements.

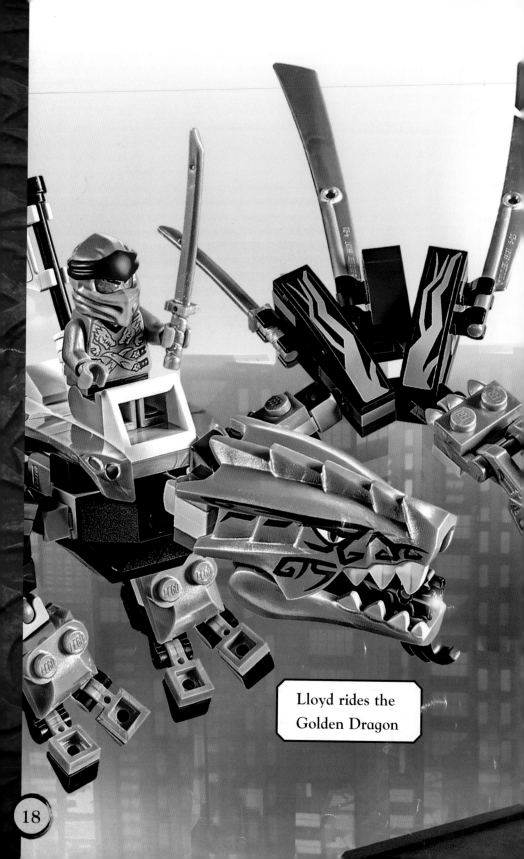

Lloyd rides the
Golden Dragon

Solo adventures

The ninja work best as a team, but they cannot stick together all the time. During their adventures they are often split up. Sometimes a ninja is forced to battle an enemy or rescue a teammate alone. These solo adventures are among the riskiest ninja missions of all.

Stone scout

Lord Garmadon

Family relationships can be difficult. Lloyd's dad, Lord Garmadon, is always attacking Ninjago. As the ninja leader, Lloyd often has to fight his own dad!

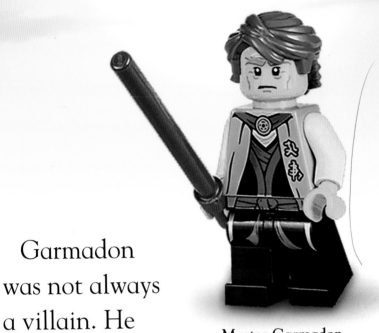

Master Garmadon

Garmadon was not always a villain. He turned bad after he was bitten by a snake called "The Great Devourer." The snake's venom made him want to rule Ninjago and boss the people around.

Once, Garmadon was briefly cured of his bad ways. He became Master Garmadon, a kind dad and patient teacher. Lloyd really bonded with him. But soon Garmadon turned bad again, and the fighting began once more.

The Sky Pirates are flying villains who menace Ninjago. Their captain is a wicked Djinn named Nadakhan. For years, Nadakhan has been trapped in the Teapot of Tyrahn. He blames the ninja! Now he is free, he wants revenge.

Nadakhan turns the ninja into statues, but somehow his magic does not work on Jay. Jay keeps on fighting.

Nadakhan

Nadakhan grants Jay three wishes, hoping to trick him into surrendering. But Jay is clever. He uses his final wish to turn back time, leaving Nadakhan stuck in the Teapot of Tyrahn again!

Master Yang is the inventor of the flying martial arts. He hopes to become immortal by trying out the Yin Blade. Instead, he becomes a ghost! Yang realizes that to return to life he must transfer the blade's curse to someone else. He picks Cole. Then he calls the ninja's old foes from the Departed Realm to help him.

Cole does not want to be a ghost. He speeds into battle in his Ultra Stealth Raider, backed up by the other ninja.

After hours of fighting, Master Yang surrenders. He decides that being a ghost is not so bad. At least, it is better than fighting the ninja!

Poor Zane! He is stuck in a grim prison called the Kryptarium. He has been blamed for a crime he did not commit.

The other prisoners are tough criminals. One is Captain Soto, a sea pirate from days of old. Another is a four-armed Giant Stone Warrior.

Kai comes to break his friend out of prison. He leaps over the fence, then smashes his way through the prison drain. Kai and Zane rush out, past the guard. They are free!

Unfortunately, so are the criminals.

When a ninja can use their Elemental Powers at the highest level, they are said to have unlocked their True Potential.

Nya

True Potential: Ability to control water
How: By realizing that she should keep trying
When: In a battle against the Preeminent

Cole

True Potential: Incredible strength
How: By mending a rift with his dad
When: After a performance at Ninjago Concert Hall

Jay

True Potential: Control over electric currents
How: By sharing his fears with Nya
When: While saving Nya from an out-of-control roller coaster

Kai

True Potential: Resistance to heat
How: By accepting that he cannot be the Green Ninja
When: After saving Lloyd from a fire

Lloyd

True Potential: Control of all five elements
How: By accepting his destiny to be the Ultimate Spinjitzu Master
When: After the Final Battle for Ninjago

Zane

True Potential: Ability to throw ice beams
How: By understanding that he is a robot
When: On a journey through a frosted forest

Undercover missions

True ninja are stealthy as well as brave.
They must move silently so enemies do
not hear them. They must hide in
shadows so enemies do not see them.

Most of all, they must know how to conceal their true identities. Missions that rely on these stealthy skills are known as undercover missions.

At first, there are only five ninja—Lloyd, Kai, Jay, Cole, and Zane. Then a mysterious warrior named Samurai X appears, fighting alongside them. The warrior pilots a huge mech and a helmet hides his or her face. Who can it be? Samurai X sends the Serpentine slithering off and makes the Skulkins scatter. Eventually, the identity of Samurai X is revealed. It is Nya, Kai's sister! Nya wants to be a ninja, too, so she has secretly trained herself to fight and built her own mech. The ninja have to agree that she has proved herself. Nya becomes the sixth ninja.

P.I.X.A.L. is an android built by Dr. Cyrus Borg. Her full name is Primary Interactive X-ternal Assistant Life-form.

P.I.X.A.L. wants to help the ninja battle their enemies, but her metal body has been scrapped by Master Chen and his criminals. She needs a new one, so she steals Nya's old Samurai X armor.

At first, Nya thinks the newcomer is an enemy in disguise. However, when P.I.X.A.L. proves her skills and reveals her identity, Nya accepts her as the new Samurai X. She lets P.I.X.A.L. keep the armor and mech—as long as she changes it from red to blue!

Lloyd's Titan
Mech

Mechs are massive, armored battle
suits that the ninja climb into
and pilot like vehicles. The ninja
upgrade their mechs often, to include
all the latest gadgets and technology.

Mechs usually reflect the color and
some of the weapons of the ninja who
pilots them. Lloyd's Titan Mech is green
and its weapons include a six-bladed
golden shuriken.

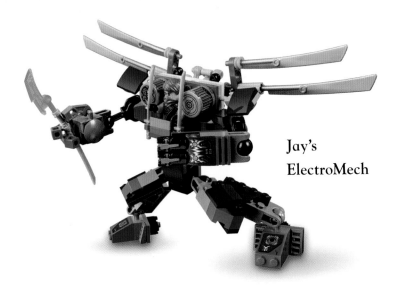

Jay's
ElectroMech

A good mech includes some surprise features. Jay's ElectroMech has flip-up swords that also act as wings.

It is not only ninja who own mechs. During his time as a bounty hunter, Ronin uses a mech with a net shooter to get foes in a tangle.

Ronin's Salvage
M.E.C.

The Sons of Garmadon are bikers with a mean mission. They want to have Lord Garmadon reborn and make him emperor of Ninjago!

Zane wants to spy on the gang. He disguises himself as a Garmadon fan named Snake Jaguar so the bikers let him into their hideout.

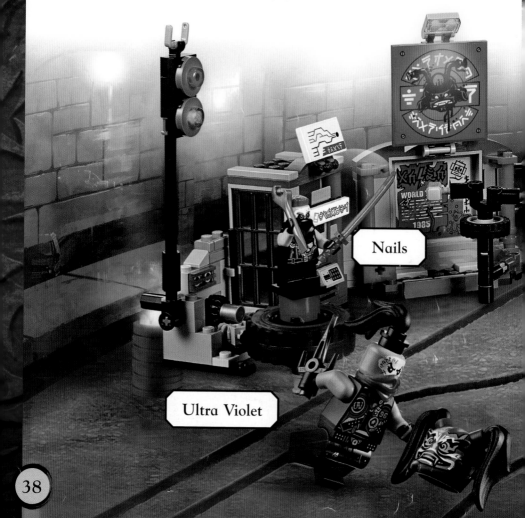

Nails

Ultra Violet

The bikers soon see through Zane's disguise. Ultra Violet, Nails, and Skip Vicious attack Zane, but Lloyd arrives in time to fight them off.

Zane escapes with Lloyd. His mission was short but successful. He has learned all the Sons of Garmadon's secret plans!

Skip Vicious

Snake Jaguar

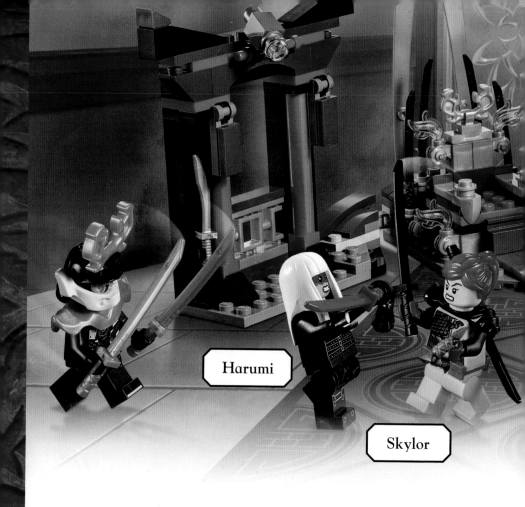

Harumi

Skylor

Sometimes the ninja's enemies go undercover, too. Princess Harumi is the adopted daughter of the Emperor and Empress of Ninjago. In public, she does kind deeds and helps the poor. In secret, she hero-worships Garmadon and plots the downfall of the ninja.

The white-haired princess is so sweet
to the ninja that Lloyd starts to fall
in love with her. He is shocked when
she suddenly turns on the ninja and
locks them up.

Harumi has forgotten that the ninja
have allies! Skylor comes looking for her
friends. She fights off Harumi and releases
the ninja from the palace prison.

It can be hard to tell friend from foe. Villains often tell lies and pretend to be good guys!

NAME: DOUBLOON
When the Sky Pirates capture Jay, crew member Doubloon pretends he has switched sides and wants to help Jay escape. It is all a trick to gain Jay's trust and destroy the ninja!

NAME: KRUX
Krux convinces the ninja he is Dr. Saunders, a museum curator. But he is a villain who is secretly breeding the Vermillion snake army to help him conquer Ninjago.

NAME: CAPTAIN SOTO

Soto is a pirate captain who returns from the past to loot Ninjago's villages. At first, he fights the ninja. Later he becomes their ally after learning that they are battling his old foes, the Sky Pirates.

NAME: PYTHOR

Pythor is the last of the Anacondrai Serpentines. He offers to be Lloyd's servant, but only to get his hands on a map that will lead him to the other Serpentine tribes.

Epic quests

The ninja are nearly always on an adventure of some kind. They never turn down a call for help, even if just one person needs their protection.

However, sometimes they face much greater challenges. Sometimes, the whole of Ninjago is under threat. When these times come, the ninja must prepare for one of their truly epic quests.

Ninjago is in peril! The nasty Serpentine serpents have released the Great Devourer. This giant snake eats everything it sees. If no one can stop it, it will eat all of Ninjago.

The Green Ninja rides the Ultra Dragon to battle the Great Devourer. This four-headed dragon is swift and strong, but the snake smashes it to the ground with a flip of its tail.

The Great Devourer

In the end, the ninja work with
Garmadon to conquer the Great Devourer.
They confuse the snake while Garmadon
uses four magical weapons to defeat it.
Just for once, Garmadon is a hero!

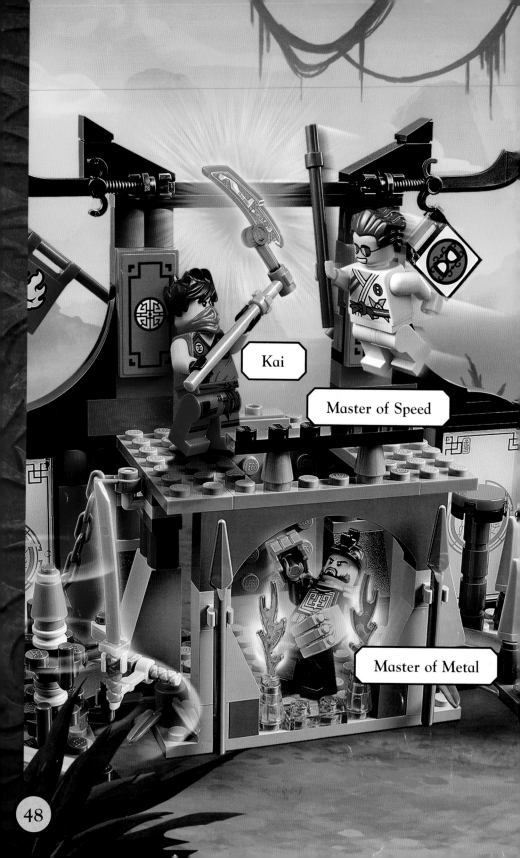

Kai

Master of Speed

Master of Metal

Master Chen is an ex-criminal. He lives in exile on a secret island, but he dreams of ruling Ninjago.

Chen invites all the Elemental Masters in Ninjago to a contest called the Tournament of Elements. He plans to steal their powers and take over Ninjago!

The ninja face many rivals at the tournament. In one fight, Kai battles the Master of Speed over a pit of fire. He does not want to fall in, like the Master of Metal!

Eventually, the ninja uncover Master Chen's plan. Kai defeats Chen and everyone gets their powers back. Ninjago is saved!

Evil Master Chen sits in his jungle temple, plotting to conquer Ninjago. He is surrounded by his loyal soldiers, fierce warrior snakes called the Anacondrai.

Chen is holding Jay in his temple prison. He plans to steal Jay's lightning powers. Lloyd rushes to rescue his friend, but he faces many dangers.

Zugu

Kapau'rai

First he must dodge drops of poison falling from a giant snake head. Then he must break Jay out of prison. Then both ninja must fight Chen's Anacondrai guards, Zugu and Kapau'rai.

The ninja defeat the guards and escape, leaving Master Chen angrily shaking his staff!

Master Chen

Acronix

Krux

Acronix and Krux are known as the Time Twins. They seek to travel to the past and remake Ninjago with themselves as rulers.

The twins pilot the Iron Doom. This huge, snake-shaped mech was built by the Vermillion—an army of slithering red snakes. The Iron Doom has a time travel device powered by four Time Blades. When the Iron Doom whizzes back through time, the ninja follow it. They mess about with the controls, sending the mech hurtling into the future with the Time Twins inside. Who knows whether the Time Twins will ever find their way back?

The Oni Titan is a huge monster as tall as a skyscraper. Garmadon builds it out of giant rocks to help him conquer Ninjago.

Even the ninja cannot stop the Oni Titan. It just keeps crushing things. It crushes Master Wu's boat, *Destiny's Bounty*. It nearly crushes Nya's armored car. It even crushes a building with Harumi inside.

In the end, it takes the ninja, their dragons, Master Wu, and some brave Ninjago citizens to bring down the Oni Titan. When Lloyd strips Garmadon of his powers, the monster crumbles into a pile of rocks.

The Dragon Hunters catch dragons and take them to their Dragon Pit. They steal the dragons' powers, and sometimes eat the poor beasts, too. To save the dragons, the ninja must get past the Dragon Pit's defenses, then battle the Dragon Hunters.

Iron Baron is the leader of the Dragon Hunters. This bully is not very popular!

Heavy Metal

Soon, a Dragon Hunter named Heavy Metal turns on Iron Baron and starts helping the ninja fight him. Before long, all the Hunters switch sides! The ninja and the Dragon Hunters defeat Iron Baron and free the dragons.

Iron Baron

The ninja never rest. They know that new enemies might arise at any time. They also know that old enemies often return! Every day, the ninja practice with their weapons and brush up on their Spinjitzu skills.

They also take care to follow Master Wu's teachings about inner strength.

None of the ninja can predict when the next adventure will begin, but there is one thing they do know. When danger threatens Ninjago, they will be ready.

Ninja, Go!

Quiz

1. What is the ninja training arena called?

2. What is the name of Lloyd's mom?

3. Where are dragons born?

4. Which ninja sometimes stops foes by piling dirt on them?

5. What happens when Master Yang tries out the Yin Blade?

6. What is the Kryptarium?

7. Who is the second Samurai X?

8. Which gang do Ultra Violet, Nails, and Skip Vicious belong to?

9. What color is Princess Harumi's hair?

10. How many heads does the Ultra Dragon have?

Answers on page 63

Glossary

ally
Someone who gives help and support.

android
A robot shaped like a human.

bounty hunter
Someone who captures outlaws in return for payment.

Djinn
A genie. Some Djinn are able to grant wishes to people.

element
A substance such as earth, water, or fire that is a part of the natural world.

exile
If someone is in exile they have been banned from living in their own country.

immortal
Living forever.

Spinjitzu
A martial art used by the ninja. It involves spinning at high speed to create a tornado of energy.

stealthy
Secretly, silently, so no one notices.

Index

Answers to the quiz on pages 60 and 61:
1. A dojo 2. Misako 3. In the First Realm 4. Cole
5. He turns into a ghost 6. A prison 7. P.I.X.A.L.
8. The Sons of Garmadon 9. White 10. Four

A LEVEL FOR EVERY READER

This book is a part of an exciting four-level reading series to support children in developing the habit of reading widely for both pleasure and information. Each book is designed to develop a child's reading skills, fluency, grammar awareness, and comprehension in order to build confidence and enjoyment when reading.

Ready for a Level 3 (Beginning to Read Alone) book

A child should:

- be able to read many words without needing to stop and break them down into sound parts.
- read smoothly, in phrases and with expression, and at a good pace.
- self-correct when a word or sentence doesn't sound right or doesn't make sense.

A valuable and shared reading experience

For many children, reading requires much effort but adult participation can make reading both fun and easier. Here are a few tips on how to use this book with a young reader:

Check out the contents together:

- read about the book on the back cover and talk about the contents page to help heighten interest and expectation.
- ask the reader to make predictions about what they think will happen next.
- talk about the information he/she might want to find out.

Encourage fluent reading:

- encourage reading aloud in fluent, expressive phrases, making full use of punctuation and thinking about the meaning; if helpful, choose a sentence to read aloud to help demonstrate reading with expression.

Praise, share, and talk:

- notice if the reader is responding to the text by self-correcting and varying his/her voice.
- encourage the reader to recall specific details after each chapter.
- let her/him pick out interesting words and discuss what they mean.
- talk about what he/she found most interesting or important and show your own enthusiasm for the book.
- read the quiz at the end of the book and encourage the reader to answer the questions, if necessary, by turning back to the relevant pages to find the answers.

Series consultant, Dr. Linda Gambrell, Distinguished Professor of Education at Clemson University, has served as President of the National Reading Conference, the College Reading Association, and the International Reading Association.